Wynken, Blynken, and Nod

Wynken, Blynken, and Nod

Written by Eugene W. Field
Illustrated by Giselle Potter

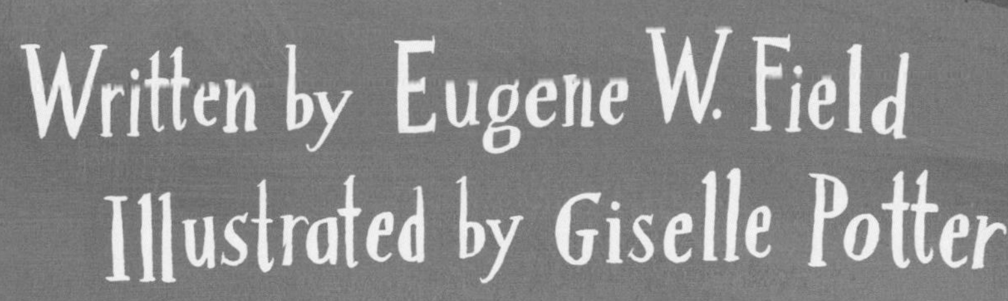

Schwartz & Wade Books
New York

Published by Schwartz & Wade Books,
an imprint of Random House Children's Books,
a division of Random House, Inc., New York.

Visit us on the Web! www.randomhouse.com/kids

Educators and librarians, for a variety of
teaching tools, visit us at
www.randomhouse.com/teachers

Library of Congress Cataloging-in-Publication Data
Field, Eugene.
Wynken, Blynken, and Nod : a Dutch lullaby / Eugene
Field ; illustrated by Giselle Potter. – 1st ed.
p. cm.
ISBN 978-0-375-84196-5 (alk. paper)–
ISBN 978-0-375-94596-0 (lib. bdg.)
1. Children's poetry, American. 2. Sleep–Juvenile
poetry. [1. Sleep–Poetry. 2. American poetry.] I. Potter,
Giselle, ill. II. Title.
PS1667.W8 2008
811'.4–dc22 2007009568

The text of this book is hand-lettered.
The illustrations are rendered in pencil, ink, gouache,
gesso, and watercolor.
Printed in China

10 9 8 7 6 5 4 3 2 1

First Edition

Random House Children's Books supports the First
Amendment and celebrates the right to read.

for Pia, Isabel, and Kier,
and thank you, Anne and Lee
-G. P.

Wynken, Blynken, and Nod one night
Sailed off in a wooden shoe ~

Sailed on a river of crystal light,
Into a sea of dew.

"Where are you going, and what do you wish?"
The old moon asked the three.

"We have come to fish for the herring fish
That live in this beautiful sea;
Nets of silver and gold have we!"

Said Wynken,
Blynken,
And Nod.

The old moon laughed and sang a song,
As they rocked in the wooden shoe,
And the wind that sped them all night long
Ruffled the waves of dew.

The little stars were the herring fish

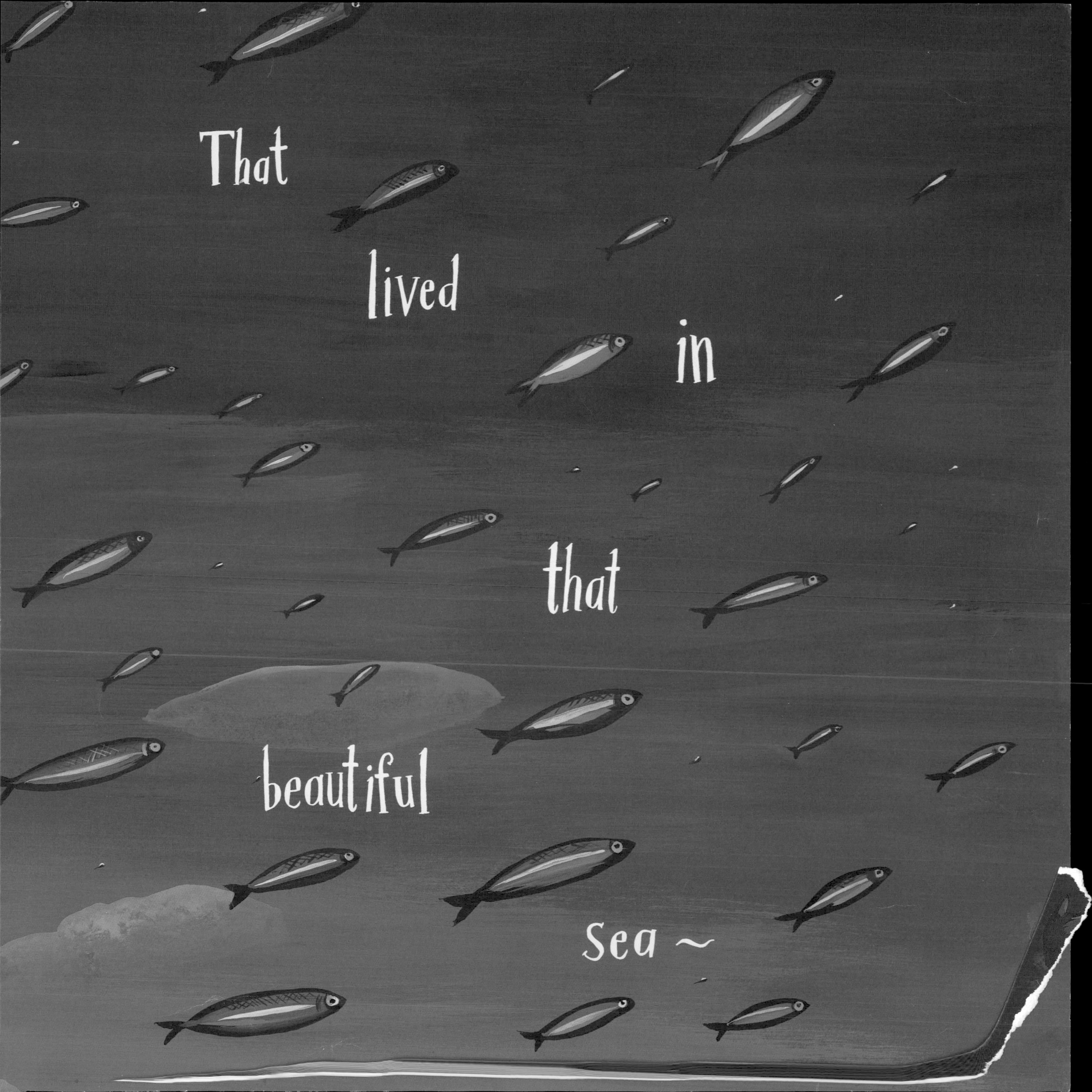

That

lived

in

that

beautiful

sea ~

"Now cast your nets wherever you wish ~
Never afeard are we";
So cried the stars to the fishermen three:
Wynken,
Blynken,
And Nod.

All night long their nets they threw
To the stars in the twinkling foam ~

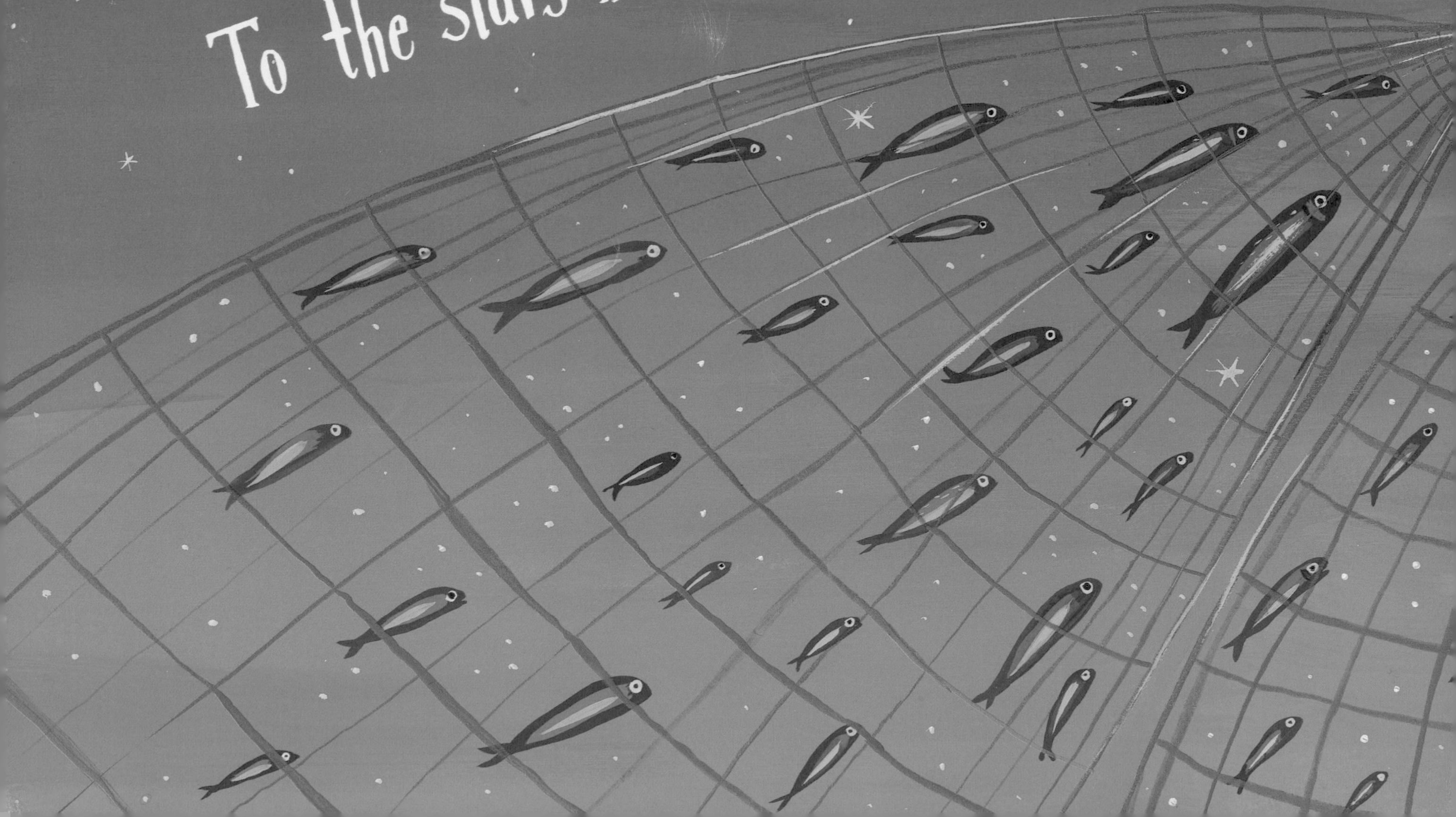

Then down from the skies
came the wooden shoe,
Bringing the fishermen home;

'Twas all so pretty a sail it seemed
As if it could not be,
And some folks thought 'twas a dream they'd dreamed
Of sailing that beautiful sea ~
But I shall name you the fishermen three:
Wynken,
Blynken,
And Nod.

Wynken and Blynken are two little eyes,
And Nod is a little head,
And the wooden shoe that sailed the skies
Is a wee one's trundle-bed.

So shut your eyes while mother sings
Of wonderful sights that be,

And you shall see the beautiful things
As you rock in the misty sea,
Where the old shoe rocked the fishermen three:

Wynken,
Blynken,
And Nod.

Illustrator's Note

When Eugene W. Field first published "Wynken, Blynken, and Nod" in 1889, the poem was called simply "Dutch Lullaby." In addition to his work as a newspaper journalist, Field wrote many poems and stories for children and came to be known as "the children's poet." He believed children should indulge their daydreams and imaginations before they must assume the responsibilities of adulthood.

As an artist, I'm always searching for words or stories that inspire me, and when I came across "Wynken, Blynken, and Nod," I was immediately attracted to it. The idea of the characters representing two eyes and a head, and of the night sky becoming a sea of fish . . . it had a strangeness that often exists in old stories and rhymes for children, a sensibility that is hard to find today. The story reminded me of the French silent movie *A Trip to the Moon,* and of the old songs my grandmother used to sing to me in her high, scratchy voice. The poem rocked and sailed around my mind for a long time before I finally decided that I needed to paint it. Although it is one of the shortest, simplest texts I've ever illustrated, it was by far the most challenging. The repetitive imagery made it very difficult to make each picture different. But in the end, I enjoy being challenged. And I loved spending time with Eugene Field's eerie "Wynken, Blynken, and Nod."